GREEK MYTHOLOGY

BOOKS FOR KIDS

Retold by Anthony Clark

Illustrated by: Robert Harper

For Beginners Publishing

Greek Mythology Books for Kids
Retold By: Anthony Clark
Illustrated By: Robert Harper
Icons and backgrounds obtained via Shutterstock.com
Copyright © 2015 For Beginners Publishing
Visit us at www.forbeginnerspublishing.com

TABLE OF CONTENTS

INTRODUCTION

The ancient Greeks didn't worship just one god. They were polytheistic, which means they worshipped many gods. The myths, or stories, involving their gods and heroes together make up what is known today as Greek mythology. Some of the myths explained why various natural phenomena occurred. For example, a lightning storm likely meant that Zeus, god of the sky, was angry. An earthquake could have been caused by Poseidon, god of the sea, striking his trident against the earth, or perhaps by his brother Hades, god of the underworld, doing the same with his pitchfork. The rising and setting of the sun occurred at the hands of the sun god, Helios, who woke early every morning to drive his fiery sun chariot across the sky.

The most powerful gods in Greek mythology were the Olympians who lived high on Mount Olympus. The twelve Olympian gods included Zeus, his wife Hera, Apollo, Aphrodite, Ares, Artemis, Athena, Demeter, Hades, Hephaestus, Hermes, and Hestia (who was replaced by Dionysus).

The Olympians gained their power by overthrowing the Titan gods who came before them. The Titans were actually the parents and grandparents of the Olympian gods. Some of the better known Titans were Uranus (heaven), Gaia (earth), Hyperion (light), Cronus (time), Atlas (strength), and Prometheus (forethought). Prometheus, who sided with the Olympians in the battle against the Titans, gained fame as the god who brought fire to mankind.

In addition to the Olympians and the Titans, Greek mythology includes stories about lesser gods and goddesses, and stories featuring bold heroes, such as Hercules, Achilles, Perseus, Odysseus, and Jason. There are also numerous stories in Greek mythology involving fearsome monsters and creatures, such as the many-headed serpent known as the Hydra, the bull-headed creature called the Minotaur, and Medusa, the Gorgon who could turn men into stone.

The ancient Greeks honored their gods through festivals and celebrations, and through art and literature. Some cities or regions in ancient Greece favored particular gods over others. There is no single book or single source for the Greek myths, and so the myths sometimes differ from one source to another. Many of the Greek gods and goddesses have counterparts in Roman mythology, and in some cases a god's Roman name may be more familiar in modern times than the Greek version. For example, the Greek god Eros is much better known today by his Roman name "Cupid."

In this book, you will familiarize yourself with three Greek stories and be introduced to brief biographies for some of the more important Greek gods and goddesses.

ARACHNE AND ATHENA

"No one can weave like I can!" the young maiden proudly declared.

The boastful girl's name was Arachne, and she was a truly talented weaver. Not only were Arachne's creations exquisite, but her manner of working was also something to behold. People came from all around Athens to watch her card the wool, twirl the spindle, weave the fabric, and embroider it with intricate patterns.

"Her designs are so fine, so perfect, they might have been crafted by Athena herself!" a man proclaimed one day as he watched Arachne work

her magic at the loom.

People had been paying young Arachne compliments for a long time, and that was the reason she'd become so boastful. But no one before today had ever compared her to the great Athena!

Others who were present gasped at the man's remark. Athena was a goddess—the goddess of wisdom. Athena was a daughter of Zeus, the ruler of all the gods. It was known that Athena was Zeus' favorite child, and, as such, she was allowed to use his weapons, including his mighty thunderbolt. It was also known that Athena had no mother, and that she'd sprung from her father's forehead fully grown and clad in battle armor.

Athena patronized warfare, but only the defensive kind. Being the goddess of wisdom, her primary concerns were activities of the mind such as reason, literature, and the arts. As a patron of the arts, Athena considered herself the master of all weavers. Most mortals would never dare to compare themselves to a god or goddess. But over the past few years, Arachne had become overly proud. Some might even say that the young maiden had grown arrogant.

"Can you say that again?" Arachne asked the

man who'd just paid her the greatest compliment she'd ever received.

The man repeated himself, saying, "Your designs are so fine, so perfect, they might have been crafted by Athena herself."

The people gathered around gasped again at the blasphemous statement.

But Arachne didn't gasp. Instead she pondered the man's words for a few moments, then turned to him and said, "You're wrong about that. Athena doesn't have the skill I do. No one can weave like I can—not even the goddess Athena!"

There was another collective gasp. One woman nearly fainted. Several people stepped aside so that they'd be well out of the way in the event Athena decided to send her father's thunderbolt crashing down.

But Athena wasn't aware of Arachne's boasts. Not yet, at least.

Some of those who'd gathered at Arachne's house to watch her work weren't humans. There were wood nymphs present who'd come in from the forest to see if the stories they'd heard about the maiden weaver were true. One of the nymphs went to tell Athena about the maiden. When

Athena heard about Arachne's boast, she was outraged.

"She said what?" The goddess's face reddened as she rose from her throne.

"She said that your skill is no match for hers," the wood nymph repeated. "She said that no one can weave like she can . . . not even the goddess Athena."

"We shall she about that," Athena said. "Tell me this maiden's name, little nymph."

"Her name is Arachne," the wood nymph replied. "She has become quite famous throughout Athens for her designs. I must admit, the young woman is truly talented."

Athena glared at the nymph. "Are you saying that you agree with her?"

"No, of course not," the nymph answered quickly. "Everyone knows that no one, mortal or immortal, can match your skill at the loom."

Athena settled back onto her throne. After a few moments, she said, "I am not a cruel goddess. I will give this maiden Arachne a chance to take back what she said."

"She's a very boastful young woman," the nymph remarked. "She may not wish to take back her words."

"If she doesn't," Athena said, "then I will show the silly girl who the superior weaver really is."

Before the nymph's eyes, Athena changed her form. No longer did she appear as the goddess she was, but instead she took on the shape of a haggard old woman. Disguised as such, Athena went to the house of Arachne and knocked on the door.

"Yes?" said the young maiden as she opened the door and beheld the old woman. "What can I do for you? Have you come to watch me weave? Perhaps you would like to purchase one of my tapestries?"

"I didn't bring along my purse," said Athena, speaking as an old woman, "so I won't be making any purchases today. But I did want to talk to you about an aspect of your work."

"Which aspect would that be?" asked Arachne. "The quality of the fabric I spin? The intricateness of the patterns I embroider into the fabric?"

"Actually, I came to talk to you about your boasting."

"My boasting?" said Arachne. "But it's not boasting if it's true! I really am the greatest weaver

who has ever lived! Anyone in Athens will tell you the same."

"That may very well be true," said Athena, still in her old woman guise. "But you were also overheard bragging that your skill surpasses that of Athena. Surely you don't really believe that. I'm certain the great goddess would forgive you if only you took back your words."

"Why would I take back my words, when they're absolutely true? I don't care if Athena is a goddess. I'm willing to challenge her to a contest any day of the week!"

"Well then, how about today?" said Athena, suddenly changing both her form and her voice. She no longer appeared as an old woman; instead, she looked youthful and vibrant, and she was dressed in beautiful flowing garments. Her voice no longer sounded like an old woman's; instead, it became full and clear.

The spectators who'd gathered to watch Arachne work gasped at the sight of the goddess. After a moment, they all dropped to their knees out of respect for the great Athena. Some of the nymphs ran off to tell others of the contest that was about to commence between Arachne and Athena—a mortal and a goddess.

Out of nowhere a loom appeared, just a few feet from the spot where Arachne's stood.

Athena gathered up her skirts and took a seat in front of her loom.

Arachne, situating herself before her own loom, said to the goddess, "And who will judge this contest?"

"The nymphs will serve as the judges," replied Athena. Then, turning toward a water nymph who was standing close by, she said, "Tell us when to begin."

"Are each of you ready?" asked the water nymph.

"You don't have to ask a goddess if she's ready," said Athena, scowling at the nymph.

Arachne nodded. "I am ready to prove that my words are true," she said. Then, raising an arm and gesturing toward the growing audience, she declared, "All of you gathered here today will bear witness to the fact that my skill is greater than that of my visitor!"

"If you're both ready," said the water nymph, "then go ahead and start weaving!"

Both Arachne and Athena got to work, each moving her shuttle back and forth with incredible

speed and precision. The threads on each loom began to combine to form fabric—tapestries of colors and patterns that rivaled any artwork by any master artist.

The designs were so amazing that the audience showed their appreciation by breaking out in spontaneous applause numerous times as the weavers worked.

Athena wove a tapestry depicting the gods and goddesses in all their glory, engaged in various heroic and important acts. Athena even depicted herself winning a contest over Poseidon, the sea god, by creating the olive tree.

Arachne chose similar subjects for her tapestry, but her approach was different. Instead of portraying the gods and goddesses as wise and heroic, she depicted their failings and shortcomings. She showed them drinking, acting foolishly, and behaving in very ungodly ways.

At first, it seemed to the audience that Athena's tapestry would turn out the better one, but after Arachne had a few minutes to settle into her work, she began to hit her stride. The spectators were amazed by her subtle use of color and the way her threads came together so flawlessly.

"The images in the maiden's tapestry," one man remarked, "are so lifelike!"

"Lifelike indeed!" echoed several others.

Finally, it became clear that Arachne's tapestry would far surpass Athena's in originality of design, level of perfection, and sheer beauty. But before the nymphs could officially declare the maiden the winner, Athena lost her temper.

"Silly girl!" Athena roared as she rose to her feet. "I will show you who is more skilled!"

Reaching out, the goddess tore Arachne's tapestry, shredding the beautiful images beyond recognition. Then, Athena struck Arachne on her head, knocking the girl back onto the floor.

For a moment everyone gathered around wondered if the angry goddess intended to take the young maiden's life. Soon, however, it became clear that Athena was not going to strike the girl dead. But it also became clear that Arachne would not escape punishment.

Pointing down at Arachne, the goddess declared, "If you like weaving so much, you can weave for the rest of eternity. From now until the end of time, your very life will depend upon your ability to weave."

Reaching down, Athena touched Arachne in the middle of her forehead and instantly, the girl began to change.

Her head began to shrink and shrivel, as did her arms and legs. After a few moments, the girl's arms and legs had shrunken so much they were no longer visible. Then, her fingers began to grow and elongate, while her thumbs fell off completely. As Arachne's head continued to shrink, her belly began to swell.

By the time her transformation was complete, Arachne no longer resembled a young maiden at all. Instead, she was a different creature altogether—a new kind of creature that no one had ever seen before.

"What has she become?" asked one of the spectators, stepping forward to have a closer look. "She is a thing with a round middle, a tiny head, and eight long fingers."

Since the people were now much larger in size than Arachne, she feared that one of them might accidentally step on her and crush her. To avoid their footfalls, she quickly scrambled up the wall, climbing all the way to the ceiling.

On the ceiling, Arachne began to spin thread

out of her body—she no longer needed a loom or supplies, as she quickly realized. The audience of humans and nymphs watched in amazement as Arachne spun a silken web that crisscrossed from one wall to another, covering a corner of the ceiling.

"What a beautiful tapestry!" exclaimed one of the onlookers.

"I think it's ugly!" declared another spectator, a woman who very clearly held cleanliness in high importance. "Unless someone else wants to do it," the woman continued, "I'm going to grab a broom and knock that web down!"

And so began Arachne's new life in her new form. As Athena had decreed, Arachne's very life—even her food supply—now depended upon her ability to weave. And even though she wove beautiful webs of intricate design, most humans saw them as ugly and bothersome. Because humans were constantly destroying her webs, Arachne was forced to weave almost nonstop just to survive.

Eventually, Arachne came to be known by the name "Arachnid." The first Arachnid, or spider, began life as a boastful young weaver—she still weaves now, but no longer has time to boast.

As for the goddess Athena, the last time anyone saw her, she was still in Athens—still weaving her fine tapestries and still punishing arrogant humans, bringing them down to their proper size.

PANDORA'S BOX

"For how long will you be chained to this rock?" Epimetheus asked his brother, Prometheus.

"I do not know," replied Prometheus. "But I do know that Zeus's wrath has no end. I believe that punishing me may not be enough for him. He may wish to punish you as well, dear brother."

"But you were the one who gave fire to the humans," said Epimetheus. "Why would Zeus have a quarrel with me?"

"Because that is how he thinks," said Prometheus. "Just be careful around Zeus. I would advise you not to accept any gifts he may offer you."

28

Epimetheus thanked his brother for the wise advice before taking his leave. It pained Epimetheus to see his brother suffer so. It was true that Prometheus had disobeyed Zeus's command. The great ruler of the gods never wished for humans to have fire. Prometheus and Epimetheus, both gods themselves, felt differently about the humans. They wished good things for humanity, and so, Prometheus stole a lightning bolt from Zeus and gave it to the humans so they could make fire. Even though his brother was guilty of disobeying Zeus, Epimetheus could never bear to visit Prometheus for long. Sometimes Zeus sent rough weather and angry ocean waves crashing against his brother. Sometimes Zeus made the sun beat down upon him. Prometheus had already been chained to the rock for a long time; it seemed to Epimetheus that his brother's punishment should be enough to satisfy any vengeful god.

But Zeus was a different kind of god. As the ruler of the gods, he didn't like to be disobeyed—neither by humans nor by other gods. Prometheus was correct in thinking that Zeus had something in mind for Epimetheus—a punishment of sorts. Nothing so violent as chaining him to a rock and pummeling him with rough weather. Zeus's plan for

Epimetheus was trickier, far more devious.

"Epimetheus, I have something for you," Zeus announced to Prometheus's brother one day.

"Something for me?" asked Epimetheus in surprise. "A gift?"

"Yes, Epimetheus, a gift," said Zeus. "I know that you've been lonely without your brother. Some of the other gods and I have created something for you that I know you're going to love."

Zeus clapped his hands and a human stepped out from behind a hedgerow. The human was different from the others on Earth; this one was soft and feminine in appearance. Never before had Epimetheus seen a human created in the image of a goddess, with the beauty and allure of a goddess.

"This is Pandora," Zeus announced. "She is a woman—the first on Earth."

"She's very beautiful," uttered Epimetheus. He found that he couldn't take his eyes off the woman's face. "She's a gift for me?"

Zeus nodded. "If you like her, you can take her as your bride."

Epimetheus recalled his brother's advice about not accepting gifts from Zeus. But what could be wrong with a gift such as this one? The

woman—Pandora—was wonderful in every way as far as Epimetheus could tell.

Zeus went on to explain that the gods had imbued her with various traits. For example, Hermes had given her speech, Apollo had granted her musical ability, and Aphrodite had gifted her with great beauty.

Epimetheus realized that he couldn't say no to Zeus's gift, for he had already fallen in love with the beautiful Pandora. Their wedding was arranged for later that day. Zeus attended the ceremony along with a cadre of other gods.

At the end of the ceremony, Zeus presented a wedding gift to the newlyweds. It was a beautiful, ornately decorated box. On top of the lid, a sign had been affixed which read: DO NOT OPEN.

"I wonder what's in the box," Pandora asked her new husband once they arrived home.

"I have no clue," said Epimetheus.

"Why didn't you ask Zeus about what's inside?" Pandora questioned her husband. "Wouldn't you like to know?"

Epimetheus shrugged. "I thought it would be rude to ask Zeus," he said. "And I'm not really concerned with the contents of that box. What difference does it make?"

Pandora reached for the box's lid, as if she were going to open it.

"What are you doing?!" snapped Epimetheus. "Don't open that! You see the warning!"

"I was just going to touch it," Pandora answered sheepishly.

Epimetheus regarded her for a long moment and then said, "I am going to see Prometheus. I will return soon. Please stay away from that box, Pandora."

Pandora did stay away from the box at first. But as the day progressed, she found herself more and more interested in the box and its mysterious contents. What Epimetheus didn't know was that the gods had bestowed another trait upon his new bride—curiosity.

At last, Pandora's curiosity overcame her. Despite the warning on the lid, she lifted it up . . .

And the contents of the box began to fly out. Those contents included disease, pestilence, hatred, envy—all of the evil things in existence.

Epimetheus returned just then and saw his wife standing over the box. He also saw what had escaped from within the box.

"Pandora!" he cried out. "Do you realize what you've done? Did you see what you released into

the world?!"

She stood before the box in tears. She felt truly sorry for what she had done, but it was too late. The evil had already begun to scatter to the four corners of the world. Life would never be the same for mankind.

As Epimetheus walked over to his wife, he noticed something remaining in the box. "Look!" he said, pointing down.

The last remaining thing emerged from the box. Both Epimetheus and Pandora watched in awe as it hovered in the air.

Uncertain of what she was looking at, Pandora asked her husband, "What is it? It's unlike any of the rest of the box's former contents."

Epimetheus knew exactly what it was, and he was relieved to see that it too was being released into the world. "It's hope," he said. "And you're right, it's unlike anything else."

After that day—the fateful day Pandora opened the box from Zeus—life became more difficult for humans the world over. They were plagued by war, disease, and suffering of all kinds. But because hope was also released into the world, life also became far more meaningful for humans. Ever since that day, humans have known that hope is enough to sustain a person through all kinds of suffering.

PHAETON AND HELIOS

"Your father's not really a god," the boy teased Phaeton. "You're making that up!"

The other boys gathered around began to laugh. "Stop it with that nonsense, Phaeton," they taunted him. "You're fully mortal, like the rest of us."

One boy, larger than the rest, stepped forward and shoved Phaeton to the ground. "Ha!" laughed the larger boy. "If you were part god, you wouldn't have allowed me to push you down."

The boys laughed more loudly. One of them came forward and put his foot on Phaeton's face.

After a few minutes, the boys grew tired of bullying Phaeton and moved on to another pursuit.

Phaeton waited until they were out of sight, and then he began to cry. Ever since he was young, his mother had told him that his father was a god—the great sun god Helios. Phaeton had mentioned it to one of the boys, not as a boast, but as a passing remark. The boy had told the others. Now, based on how the boys had reacted, Phaeton wondered himself if it was true or not. Had his mother been lying to him all these years?

Phaeton went home to see his mother. "Is it really true?" he demanded. "Is my father a god?"

"It's true," replied his mother, Clymene.

"Prove it to me!"

"How can I prove it, son? Perhaps it's time for you to go meet him yourself. You're old enough to travel alone. You'll find your father's palace in the East."

Phaeton's mother gave him directions to Helios's palace. The boy packed a few items and set off due east.

Phaeton had always known that his father's duties were very demanding; that was the reason neither Phaeton nor his mother had been invited to live at the palace. Every morning, Helios had to rise early, tether his powerful steeds to the sun chariot, and drive it across the sky. There was never a day off for Helios, for if the sun chariot failed to cross the sky even one day, the balance of life on Earth would be disturbed.

It took Phaeton some time to reach his father's palace. As he approached the gates, he gaped in awe at the palace's beauty.

He tried the gates and found them open. Letting himself in, Phaeton strolled up a massive golden staircase, which led to the palace doors.

He pushed the doors open and marveled at a chamber that matched the palace's exterior beauty and design. In the rear of the chamber sat a large golden throne, which was empty at the moment. There were, however, several attendants gathered in the throne room. Phaeton recognized a few of them. Hour, Day, Week, Month, and Year were there, as were all four of the Seasons.

Just then, Phaeton heard footsteps and then saw another figure enter the throne room. There was no doubt in the boy's mind that this was the great sun god Helios, his father.

Helios was tall and powerfully built, as one would expect of a god. There was a glow about him, as if he'd bathed himself in liquid bronze. Noticing the boy, Helios smiled.

"I thought you would come one day."

"You recognize me?" asked Phaeton.

"Indeed. You are my son. I would never forget you."

"Then it's really true!" Phaeton said excitedly. "I am the son of a god!"

"Yes." Helios nodded. "Did you have a reason to doubt it?"

Phaeton told his father about the boys who had teased him. "I want to prove to them, to everyone, that you're my father."

"How will you do that?" asked Helios.

"By doing what you do, Father."

The god furrowed his brows. "What I do? You mean you want to drive the sun chariot?"

"Yes, Father. I've always dreamt of it, ever since I was young. I've always wanted to follow in your footsteps and drive the sun chariot across the sky."

"No." Helios shook his head sharply. "I'm afraid that's not possible. My horses are far too powerful. I am the only one in the universe who can keep them under control. Even mighty Zeus does not dare attempt to drive the sun chariot!"

"But, Father . . . you must allow me to drive the sun chariot at least once. I've driven chariots across the Earth many times. Surely driving a chariot across the sky isn't much different."

Helios explained that the differences were vast. But Phaeton would not give up. He continued to plead with his father until finally the sun god relented.

"Tomorrow, you will accompany me on my ride," Helios told his son, "and you will watch me closely. I'll teach you all that I can."

Phaeton stayed at the palace overnight in a guest chamber. He rose early the next morning and watched his father tether the horses to the sun chariot. His father was right: the steeds were the most powerful creatures the boy had ever set eyes upon. There were four of them; each breathed smoke, and when they walked, sparks flew off their heels.

The sun chariot was also a sight to behold. The chariot glowed so brightly that Phaeton found it impossible to gaze directly upon it. Helios helped the boy coat his skin in a bronze-colored powder, which, his father explained, would protect him from the heat from the chariot.

Stepping into the chariot, Helios took up his team's reins. Phaeton stood beside his father and watched as the sun god started moving the chariot forward. The horses ran on the Earth for only a few feet, and then they leapt into the sky, pulling the

sun chariot off the ground.

"I can't believe how fast we're moving!" Phaeton cried out as the chariot raced into the heavens.

"We have a lot of sky to cover in one day," Helios said.

"When it's my turn to drive the chariot," said Phaeton, "how will I know which way to steer the horses?"

"The horses know the way. But you have to keep them under control. You must keep them moving forward, which means you must stay focused. If you allow your mind to wander for even a few moments, you'll likely lose control of the horses. If you lose control, they may veer off course."

"What would happen if the horses veer off course?"

Helios grunted. "That would be very bad. You must not allow that to happen."

The ride across the heavens was the most thrilling thing young Phaeton had ever done. At the end of the night, he again bedded down in one of the palace's guest chambers. But he couldn't sleep a wink. He couldn't stop thinking about the coming day when he would drive the sun chariot across the sky all on his own.

After he awakened, Phaeton covered his body in the bronze powder and went out to the chariot house. His father was already there, tethering the team to the chariot.

"How about I come with you?" Helios suggested. "Just in case anything goes wrong."

"Nothing will go wrong," Phaeton said. "You taught me well, Father. Besides, if you come along, you'll be constantly tempted to take the reins from my hands. I would like to drive the chariot on my own . . . just the way you do it, Father."

The sun god sighed and nodded. "Remember everything I told you," he said as he watched his son step into the chariot and take up the reins.

"Don't worry about me, Father. That's Mother's job."

Phaeton took in a deep breath, then whispered to himself, "Here we go."

He started moving the team forward. The horses blew smoke and steam from their nostrils, and as they began moving, a shower of sparks flew from their heels.

When they leapt into the sky, Phaeton felt giddy with excitement. This is the greatest feeling ever! he thought as he watched the buildings and trees shrink in the distance beneath him.

He drove the sun chariot as his father had instructed, with a firm hand so that the team would know who was in charge. He kept his mind focused on keeping the horse team on course.

Phaeton made it a quarter of the way across the sky without incident. Then, something happened.

A shooting star passed close by, distracting young Phaeton. When he looked in the direction of the shooting star, he noticed all the other stars winking and glittering like jewels scattered across the heavens.

"Goodness," Phaeton murmured to himself. "I've never seen anything so beautiful!"

The sight of the stars up close was so dazzling that Phaeton stared at the display for several moments.

By the time he faced forward again, the team had strayed from the designated course. The sun chariot, Phaeton realized with horror, was hurtling directly toward Earth.

He pulled up on the reins, and the horses lifted their snouts and began heading skyward again. But the sun chariot had come so close to the Earth that it had scorched the trees and grass, leaving nothing but bare soil and sand. Phaeton recognized the area as a place called the Middle East. The fire caused by the sun chariot was so great that it spread to the northern part of a place called Africa, turning that area to desert as well.

With the horse team pointed skyward, the chariot shot toward the heavens like a shooting start traveling in reverse. The sun chariot drew so far from some parts of the Earth that they froze due to the lack of heat.

Phaeton realized that he had no control over the

horse team. The powerful steeds pulled the chariot in one direction, and then another, and then yet another.

"I have failed miserably," Phaeton muttered to himself. "I should've listened to my father. I should've allowed him to come along."

The ruler of all the gods, Zeus, became aware of what was occurring when he heard nymphs crying out from the burning places and the frozen places on Earth.

"This madness must stop!" Zeus bellowed as he drew out a thunderbolt.

Holding the thunderbolt high overhead, the great god aimed carefully, focusing on the bouncing, leaping, zig-zagging chariot.

Zeus let the thunderbolt fly, and it shot across the canopy of the heavens, striking Phaeton and the sun chariot from the sky.

The people on Earth pointed as they watched Phaeton and the chariot fall from the heavens; most of them assumed they were witnessing a shooting star. If they'd had a closer look, they would have seen Phaeton's hair ablaze as he streaked down through the clouds and splashed down into the river Eridanos.

The water nymphs pulled Phaeton's smoldering

body from the river and buried him on shore.

Helios grieved for some time over the loss of his son. "A chariot and a horse team can be replaced," the sun god told his attendants. "But a son is irreplaceable."

Zeus was sorry for having struck down Phaeton. "I had no choice," the ruler of the gods explained to

Helios. "Your son might have destroyed the entire Earth with the sun chariot."

Helios nodded. "I know you did what you had to," he told Zeus. "I should have taught him better."

"Your son was brave for daring to drive the sun chariot on his own," Zeus said after a moment's reflection. "He liked being in the heavens—I think that's where he should be for the rest of eternity."

Helios watched as Zeus took Phaeton from the ground where the nymphs had buried him, and placed him up among the stars.

"From now on, Phaeton will be a constellation," Zeus proclaimed. "He will be known as Auriga . . . the Charioteer."

Helios smiled at the mighty god. "I think that is very fitting," he said, turning toward the new constellation. "Now, I can gaze upon my son every time I drive my chariot across the sky."

MEET
THE OLYMPIANS, TITANS,
AND OTHER GODS

APHRODITE

Aphrodite is the Greek goddess of love, beauty, and desire. It's said that Aphrodite walked out of the sea, appearing when Cronus cut off a body part of his father, Uranus, and tossed it into the foamy waters. According to another story, Aphrodite was the daughter of Zeus and Dione.

Whatever her origin, Aphrodite was so beautifuland desirable that some gods feared she may cause a rivalry among them. To prevent a war among the gods, Zeus married Aphrodite to Hephaestus, the blacksmith of the gods. Though Hephaestus was a god himself, he wasn't seen as a threat because he was so ugly and deformed.

Hephaestus made a girdle for his wife, which turned out to be magical. Whenever Aphrodite wore the girdle she became irresistible to men and male gods. Aphrodite had many lovers, including the gods Ares and Adonis.

In Roman mythology, Aphrodite is known as Venus, and she's associated with that planet.

APOLLO

Apollo, one of the more important Greek gods, is the god of light, truth, healing, music, and poetry. Apollo is also the god of prophecy, or fortune telling. As such, he was worshipped at Delphi, where he slew the dragon known as Python.

A son of Zeus and the Titan goddess Leto, Apollo

is known as the archer, and is often depicted with his silver bow and arrows. The Greeks believed that Apollo could bring about disease and plague with his arrows, but he could also bring about healing, particularly in men. Since he is the god of music, Apollo is also sometimes depicted in artwork playing a golden lyre, which is a small U-shaped harp.

In some stories, Apollo is responsible for driving the sun chariot across the sky every day. In other versions of the mythology, that job belongs to the sun god Helios.

ARES

Ares is the Greek god of war and manly courage. A son of Zeus and Hera, Ares was one of the twelve Olympians who lived atop Mount Olympus. He usually represents the untamed, violent aspects of war rather than the disciplined, strategic aspects, which are typically attributed to the goddess

Athena.

Ares had an affair with Aphrodite and was trapped in a net laid by her husband Hephaestus, the god's blacksmith. In another story, Ares became jealous of Adonis, who also loved Aphrodite, and killed him while disguised as a boar. In the Trojan War, Ares was wounded in battle by Diomedes.

Ares is known as Mars in Roman mythology.

ARTEMIS

Artemis is the Greek goddess of the hunt, the wilderness, childbirth, and virginity. A daughter of Zeus and the Titan goddess Leto, Artemis was the twin of the god Apollo. Artemis is often depicted in artwork as a huntress armed with a bow and arrows. She was a protector of girls and was responsible for both causing and healing disease in women.

For some period of time, Artemis loved the god Orion, who was her hunting companion. There are many versions of the mythology of Artemis and Orion. In one version, Artemis is tricked into killing Orion by her brother Apollo, who wished to protect his sister's virtue. In another version, Artemis kills Orion in self-defense.

One of Artemis' symbols is the wild boar. In one story, she sent a boar to kill Adonis. In another version of the story it was Ares, disguised as a boar, who slew Adonis.

Artemis played a role in the Trojan War. Siding with the Trojans, Artemis calmed the winds to prevent the Greeks from sailing for Troy. She also took part in, and lost, a fight with Hera, the supreme goddess and wife of Zeus.

ATHENA

Athena, the Greek goddess of wisdom, was a daughter of Zeus. It was known that Athena was Zeus' favorite child, and, as such, she was allowed to use his weapons, including his mighty thunderbolt. It was also known that Athena had no mother. Instead of being born, she sprang from her father's forehead fully grown and clad in battle armor.

Athena patronized warfare, but only the defensive kind. As the goddess of wisdom, her primary concerns were activities of the mind such as reason, mathematics, literature, and the arts. Being a patron of the arts, Athena considered herself the master of all weavers. One famous story involves Athena entering a weaving contest with Arachne, a talented young woman who was transformed by Athena into the first spider in the world's history.

Athena helped several famous heroes in their quests, including Jason, Odysseus, and Hercules. She beat out the sea god Poseidon to become the patron deity of the city of Athens.

Athena is the equivalent of Minerva in Roman mythology.

HADES

Hades, the Greek god of the underworld, was the son of Cronus and the brother of Zeus and the sea god Poseidon. Though Hades was the ruler of the dead, he was not death itself. That honor went to a god named Thanatos.

Hades also became known as the god of wealth,

and was considered greedy by the ancient Greeks. He became angry with anyone who tried to cheat death or escape the underworld. He could create earthquakes with his weapon, the pitchfork.

Hades married Persephone after kidnapping her and carrying her to the underworld. Because the ancient Greeks were afraid to say his name, Hades was given several other names, the most well-known being Plouton, which the Romans Latinized as "Pluto."

HEPHAESTUS

Hephaestus is the Greek god of blacksmiths, metallurgy, fire, and volcanoes. In one version of his origin, Hephaestus is the offspring of Zeus and Hera. In another, Hera bears him alone and throws him from Mount Olympus due to his deformity. After landing in the ocean, he is raised by Thetis and

Eurynome.

In another version of the mythology of Hephaestus, he receives a disfiguring injury when he attempts to protect his mother from Zeus' advances. In this version, Zeus flings Hephaestus from Olympus, and Hephaestus lands on Lemnos, an island where he learns his blacksmithing skills. Hephaestus returns to Olympus where he becomes the blacksmith of the gods and thus, the crafter of the gods' weapons.

Because of Hephaestus' ugliness and deformity, Zeus joined him with Aphrodite, the goddess of love and beauty, in an attempt to prevent disharmony among the other gods who desired the beautiful Aphrodite.

The Roman name for the god Hephaestus is Vulcan.

HERA

As Zeus' wife, Hera is referred to as the supreme goddess. She is also known as the goddess of women and marriage.

Even though she was the protector of married women, Hera had a stormy marriage herself. Zeus courted Hera in the beginning, but when she failed to return his interest, Zeus tricked her into marrying him.

At one point in their marriage, Hera convinced several other gods to join her in a revolt against Zeus. Their revolt attempt failed, and Hera promised to never rebel against her husband again. She never attempted another revolt, but she did at times interfere with Zeus' schemes. Hera was jealous over Zeus' relationships with other females, and she spent much of her time plotting revenge against the parties involved.

HERMES

Hermes, one of the twelve Olympians, is best known as the messenger of the gods. The son of Zeus and the nymph Maia, Hermes is the god of travel, shepherds, commerce, thieves, orators, and athletes.

According to legend, Hermes constructed the

first lyre out of a hollow tortoise shell and cow intestines. Hermes also invented the pan-pipes and the flute. Renowned for his athleticism and swiftness, Hermes created the sports of boxing and foot racing.

Hermes' duties included escorting the souls of dead mortals to the underworld and carrying dreams to sleeping humans.

Hermes' children included Hermaphroditus and Pan, the famous half-man, half-goat creature from Greek mythology.

In Roman mythology, Hermes is known by the name Mercury.

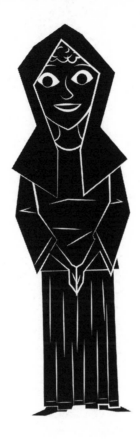

HESTIA

Hestia is the Greek goddess of the home, the hearth, family, domestic life, architecture, and the state. A daughter of the Titans Cronus and Rhea and sister of Zeus, Hestia was originally an Olympian god, but was replaced on Mount Olympus by Dionysus.

Hestia was courted by both Apollo and Poseidon, but she refused their advances and never married.

One of Hestia's duties was to keep the fires of the Olympian hearth burning. She was therefore unable to take part in the gods' processions.

POSEIDON

Poseidon is the Greek god of the sea. A son of the Titan Cronus and brother of Zeus and Hades, he was one of the twelve Olympians. According to the mythology, Poseidon drew lots with Zeus and Hades to split up the universe, and that was how Poseidon became ruler of the sea.

In an attempt to impress Demeter, the goddess of agriculture, Poseidon created the first horse (even though he was the sea god, he was also referred to as the tamer of horses). Like his brother Hades, Poseidon was considered greedy. The ancient Greeks also saw him as having a difficult personality. With his weapon, the trident, he could bring about earthquakes, just as Hades could with his pitchfork.

Poseidon was the protector of many Hellenic cities, but he lost the contest for the patronage of Athens to Athena, the goddess of wisdom. As the lord of the sea, Poseidon was the protector of the many creatures of the sea and was worshipped by sailors.

In Roman mythology, Poseidon is known as Neptune.

ZEUS

Zeus, the Greek god of the sky and ruler of the Olympians, led the Olympian gods in overthrowing the elder gods, the Titans. After winning the battle, Zeus cast most of the Titans into the pit of Tartaros.

Zeus' brothers included Poseidon, god of the sea, and Hades, god of the underworld. Zeus drew lots with his brothers to divide the universe, which was how Zeus became the ruler of the sky and king of all the gods.

As the sky god, Zeus could use his shield, Aegis, to create rain, storms, darkness, and other phenomena that are associated with the sky. The thunderbolt was Zeus' weapon, and he was known to hurl it at anyone who angered him or acted against his wishes.

Zeus was married to Hera, the supreme goddess, but he had many other relationships with goddesses and female mortals. Zeus fathered numerous offspring, many of them playing major roles in Greek mythology. These include Ares, Athena, Apollo, Hermes, Hephaestus, Persephone, Dionysus, Hercules, and Helen of Troy, among others.

Zeus is known in Roman mythology as Jupiter.

ATLAS

Atlas is one of the Titans of Greek mythology, best known for bearing the heavens on his shoulders. According to legend, Atlas led the Titans in the battle against Zeus and the Olympians. As a punishment for his role in the battle, Atlas was forced by Zeus to stand at the edge of the earth and hold the heavens on his shoulders. (Many people believe that Atlas was condemned to carry the planet on his shoulders, but his job was actually to bear the celestial globe, or to keep the heavens apart from the earth.)

Atlas is known as the Greek god of strength, and also the god of astronomy and navigation. He was responsible for turning the heavens and causing the stars to revolve.

In one famous legend, Atlas tried to trick Hercules into taking his burden—that of bearing the weight of the heavens. Hercules took the celestial globe onto his shoulders for a brief time before tricking Atlas into reclaiming his burden.

ASTRAEUS

Astraeus was the Titan god of the dusk, in addition to being god of the stars, planets, and astrology. Astraeus was also associated with winds.

Astraeus was the husband of Eos, goddess of the dawn. Together they had several children, including the four Anemoi, or winds, and the five wandering stars, Phainon, Phaethon, Pyroeis, Eosphoros/Hespersos and Stilbon (these "wandering stars" represent the planets Saturn, Jupiter, Mars, Venus, and Mercury).

Astraeus also had one daughter with Eos, Astraia, who in some sources is known as the goddess of innocence and in other sources as the goddess of the constellation Virgo.

EOS

Eos, goddess of the dawn, was a daughter of the Titans Hyperion and Theia. Her siblings were Helios, god of the sun, and Selene, goddess of the moon.

Eos' husband was Astraeus, god of the dusk, stars, planets, and astrology. With her husband, Eos had numerous children, including the four Anemoi, or winds, and the five wandering stars, or planets.

Eos, with her rose-colored fingers, rose into the sky every morning from the river Okeanos. The goddess of the dawn had many lovers, including Orion, Phaeton, and the Trojan prince Tithonos. At one point, Eos asked Zeus to make Tithonos immortal. Zeus granted the request, but Eos forgot to ask Zeus for eternal youth for Tithonos, and so, according to legend, the prince eventually shriveled up and turned into a grasshopper.

HYPERION

Hyperion, a son of Uranus and Gaia (heaven and earth), is the Titan god of light. He was also known as the Titan pillar of the east, one of the four pillars that separated the heavens from the earth.

One famous myth involves Hyperion plotting with his brothers Iapetus, Coeus, Crius, and Cronus to overthrow their father, Uranus. Later, Hyperion was among the Titan gods who were defeated by Zeus and the Olympians and cast into the pit of Tartaros.

Hyperion and his wife Theia had three children: Helios, Selene, and Eos, who represent the sun, the moon, and the dawn, respectively.

ANEMOI

The Anemoi, the offspring of Astraeus and Eos, are the four wind gods. Each of the Anemoi represents a different direction: Eurus is the east wind, Notos is the south wind, Zephryos is the west wind, and Boreas is the north wind.

Three of the Anemoi are also associated with

seasons: Notos with summer, Zephryos with spring, and Boreas with winter. Eurus isn't associated with any of the three Greek seasons.

Sometimes, the Anemoi were depicted in artwork as winged gods having human forms, and other times they were shown as horse-like beings.

In some versions of the mythology, the Anemoi are distinguished from the Anemoi Thuellai, which include storm winds and hurricanes.

EROS

In some versions of Greek mythology, Eros is presented as a primordial god, meaning that he came into being at the beginning of the universe. In other versions, he's presented as the offspring of Aphrodite. Whatever his origin, Eros is the god of love. Armed with a bow and an arrow, or flaming torch, Eros spent his days and nights causing mortals and gods alike to fall in love.

In one famous story, Aphrodite, jealous of the beautiful princess Psyche, sent Eros on a mission to make Psyche fall in love with the ugliest human being on the earth. Instead, Eros fell in love with Psyche, which ignited a drama involving Eros, Psyche, Aphrodite, and Psyche's sisters. In the end, Eros married Psyche and raised children with her.

In Roman mythology, Eros is known by the name Cupid.

NIKE

Nike, a daughter of the Titan Pallas and the goddess Styx, is the Greek goddess of victory. She and her siblings became attendants to Zeus, accompanying him into battle against the Titans. Nike's siblings, Kratos, Bia, and Zelus represented strength, force, and zeal, respectively.

As the divine charioteer, Nike's most important duty was to fly over battlefields granting glory and fame to the victors.

PHOBOS

Phobos is the Greek god of fear and panic, who often worked in tandem with his twin brother, Deimos, the god of terror and dread.

Both Phobos and Deimos were known to accompany their father, Ares, the god of war, into battle. Driving their father's chariot, Phobos and

Deimos went about spreading dread, fear, terror, and panic over any battlefield they crossed.

The twins' mother was Aphrodite, the goddess of love and beauty. Phobos and Deimos also personify the fear of loss.

Made in the USA
Middletown, DE
08 May 2016